MINE!

WRITTEN BY
CANDACE FLEMING

ILLUSTRATED BY
ERIC ROHMANN

a·s·b
anne schwartz books

In a tall, tall tree,
at the tip-tippy top,
hung a single red apple,
just about to drop.

Along skittered Mouse.

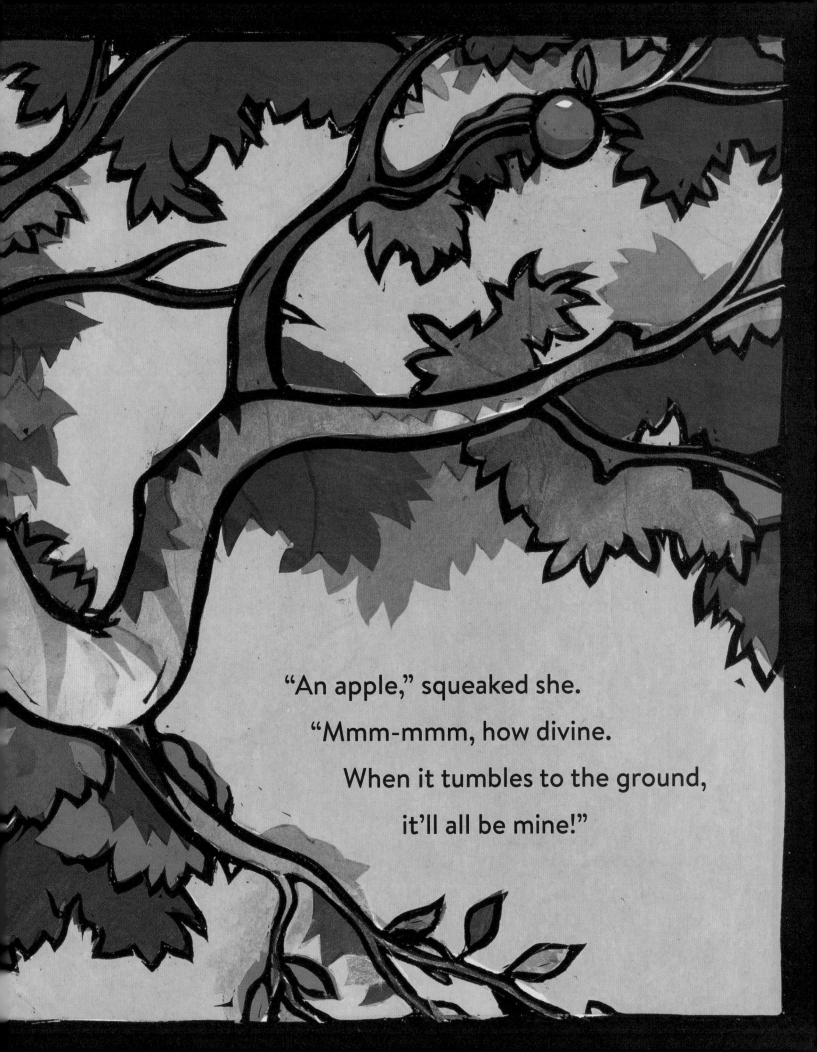

"An apple," squeaked she.

"Mmm-mmm, how divine.

When it tumbles to the ground,

it'll all be mine!"

And she zippety-eeked
beneath a fallen leaf to wait.

Along bounced Hare.

"Looky there," sniffed he.

"A crisp, crunchy lunch.

Every bite meant for me

to nibble, nabble, munch!"

And he hoppety-boinged
into the tall grass to wait.

MINE!

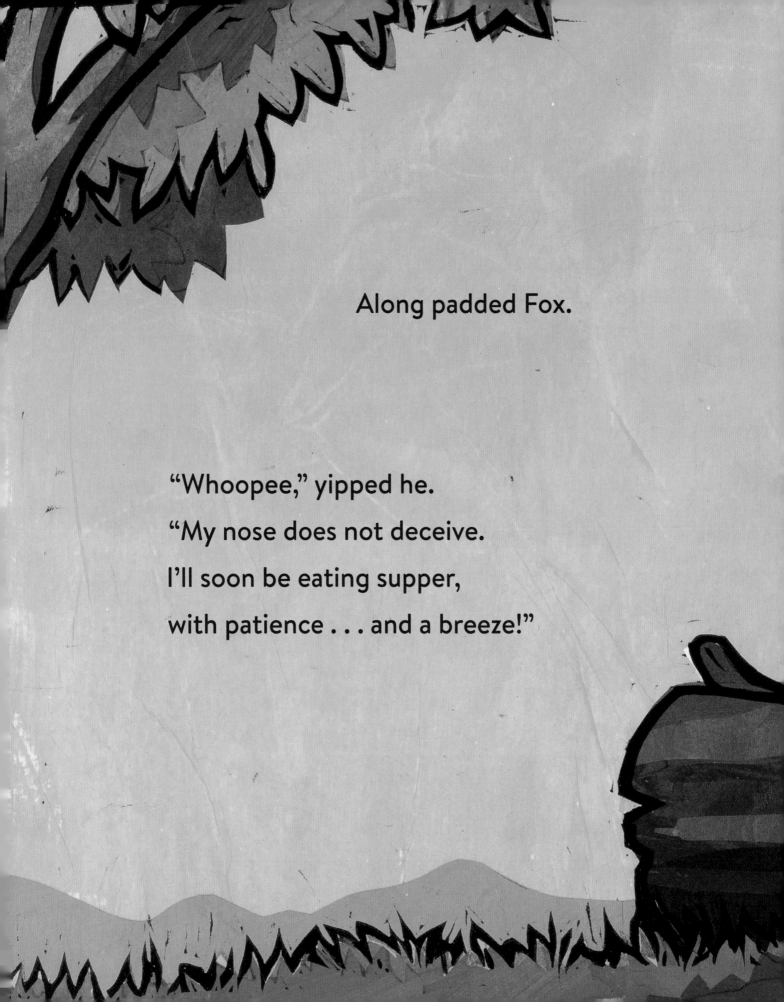

Along padded Fox.

"Whoopee," yipped he.
"My nose does not deceive.
I'll soon be eating supper,
with patience . . . and a breeze!"

And he waggety-dashed

into a hollow log to wait.

Along trotted Deer.

"Dee-licious," chuffed she.
"Juicy, red, and sweet.
Come down, Mr. Apple,
this tummy needs a treat!"

And she trippety-skipped
into a thorny bush to wait.

Along lumbered Bear.

"Nummy nums," growled he.

"See that hanging there?

My snack, my bite, my morsel.

No way I'm gonna share."

And he stompety-flopped
behind a pile of rocks to wait.

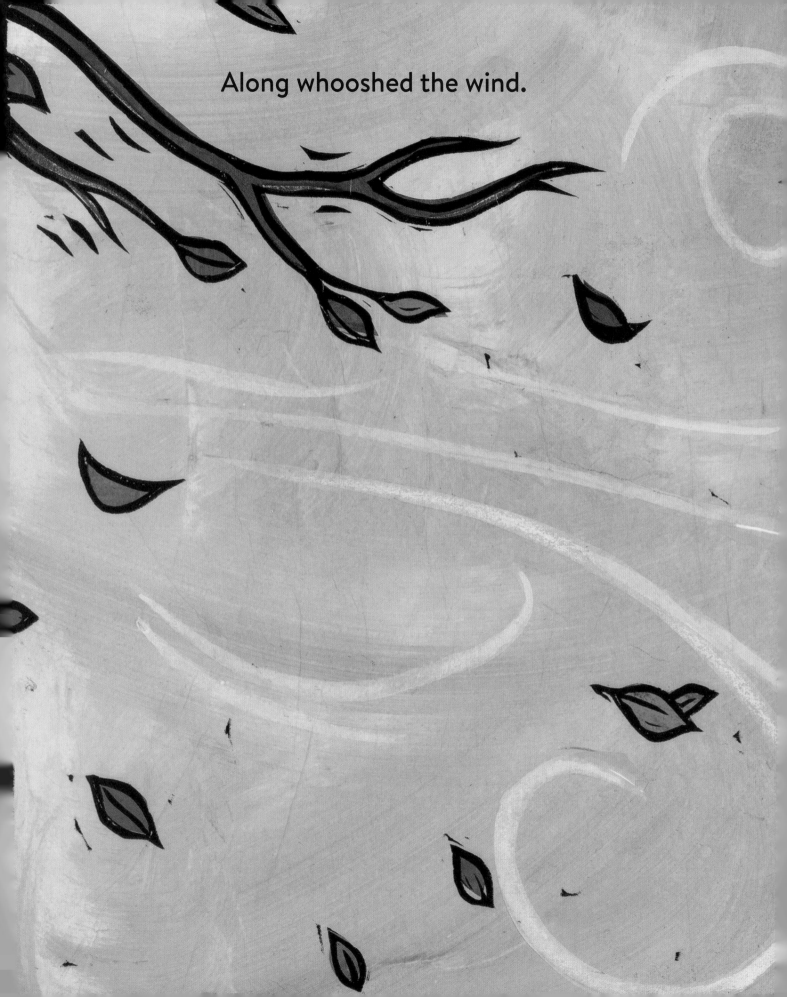

Along whooshed the wind.

"Woooo," huffed the wind.
The tree began to sway.
"Ooooh," puffed the wind.

SNAP!

The apple broke away.

Out darted Mouse.
Out bolted Hare.
Out bounded Fox,
then Deer,
then Bear.

For Archie, the apple of our eyes
—C.F. & E.R.

Text copyright © 2023 by Candace Fleming

Jacket art and interior illustrations copyright © 2023 by Eric Rohmann

All rights reserved. Published in the United States by Anne Schwartz Books,

an imprint of Random House Children's Books, a division of Penguin Random House LLC, New York.

Anne Schwartz Books and the colophon are trademarks of Penguin Random House LLC.

Visit us on the Web! rhcbooks.com

Educators and librarians, for a variety of teaching tools, visit us at RHTeachersLibrarians.com

Library of Congress Cataloging-in-Publication Data is available upon request.

ISBN 978-0-593-18166-9 (trade) — ISBN 978-0-593-18167-6 (lib. bdg.) — ISBN 978-0-593-18168-3 (ebook)

The text of this book is set in 21-point Brandon Text.

The illustrations were rendered with stained paper and relief printmaking.

Book design by Sarah Hokanson

MANUFACTURED IN CHINA 10 9 8 7 6 5 4 3 2 1 First Edition